In loving memory of Philemon, my muse —J. S. G. S.

For Freddy and Collin —S. H.

Henry Holt and Company, LLC
Publishers since 1866
175 Fifth Avenue
New York, New York 10010
mackids.com

Henry Holt® is a registered trademark of Henry Holt and Company, LLC.
Text copyright © 2013 by Judy Sue Goodwin Sturges
Illustrations copyright © 2013 by Shari Halpern

Library of Congress Cataloging-in-Publication Data
Goodwin-Sturges, Judy Sue.
Construction Kitties / by Judy Sue Goodwin Sturges ; illustrated by Shari Halpern. — 1st ed.
p.   cm.
"Christy Ottaviano Books."
Summary: Wearing their hats, Construction Kitties use heavy equipment to dig, move, push, and smooth the dirt.
ISBN 978-0-8050-9105-2 (hc)
[1. Construction equipment—Fiction. 2. Trucks—Fiction.] I. Halpern, Shari, ill. II. Title.
PZ7.G6275Con 2013   [E]—dc23   2011043537

First Edition—2013 / Designed by Ashley Halsey
The artist used gouache on Bristol board to create the illustrations for this book.
Printed in China by Macmillan Production Asia Ltd., Kwun Tong, Kowloon, Hong Kong (vendor code: PS)

1 3 5 7 9 10 8 6 4 2

Construction Kitties

Judy Sue Goodwin Sturges

illustrated by **Shari Halpern**

Christy Ottaviano Books
Henry Holt and Company • New York

The sun is up.
Time for work.
Construction Kitties
grab their hats.

Into their trucks.
Over hills, over bridges.

Onto the long, winding highway.
Construction Kitties purr
and sing to the music.

We're here!
On with our hats!
Let's get to work!

Into the loader.
Onto the excavator.
Dig that dirt!

Into the dump truck.
Onto the backhoe.

Move that dirt!

The sun is high.
Time for lunch.

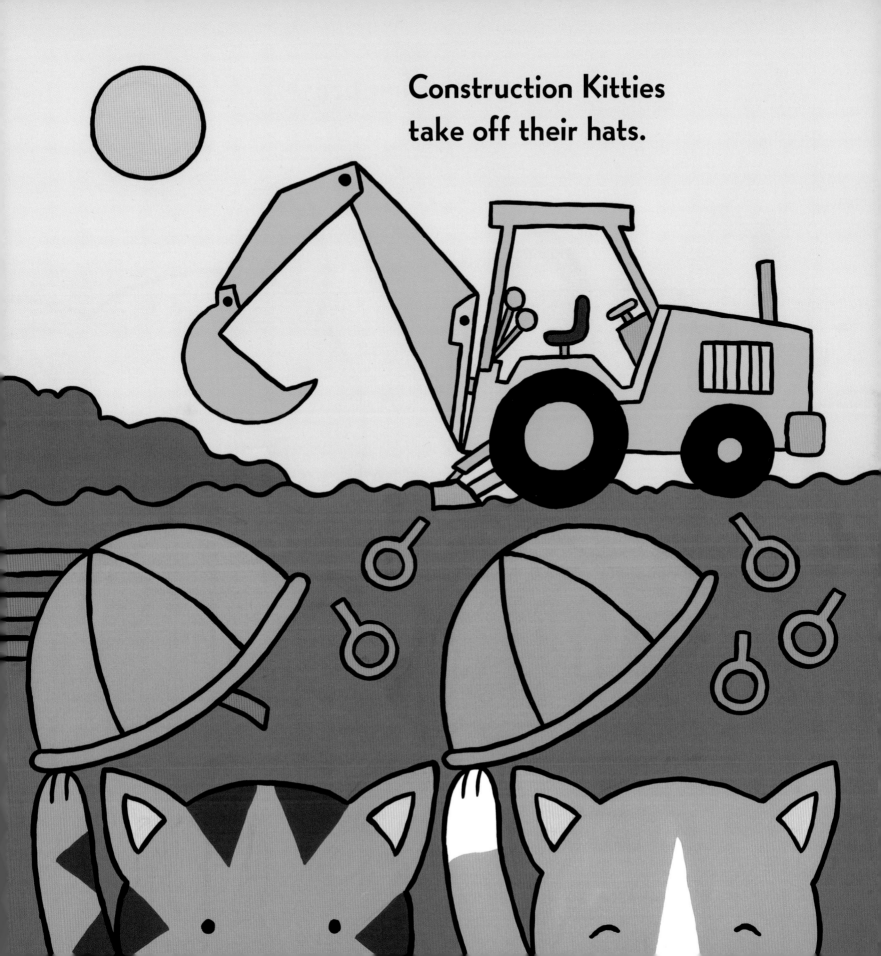

Construction Kitties
take off their hats.

Out with their pails.

Tasty sardines.
Cool milk.

Tummies are full.

Construction Kitties purr and rest.

Lots to do!
On with our hats!
Back to work!

Into the crawler.
Onto the dozer.
Push that dirt!

Into the grader.
Onto the roller.
Smooth that dirt!

The sun is low.
Time to go.

Construction Kitties
take off their hats.
A job well done.

Into their trucks.
Over hills, over bridges.
Onto the long, winding highway.

Construction Kitties purr
and sing to the music.
Soon it will be time to play!